A GOLDEN BOOK • NEW YORK

Puss in Boots copyright © 1952, renewed 1980 by Penguin Random House LLC.
The Little Red Hen copyright © 1954, renewed 1982 by Penguin Random House LLC.
The Three Bears copyright © 1948, renewed 1975 by Penguin Random House LLC.

Library of Congress Control Number: 2014952980
ISBN 978-0-553-53667-6
MANUFACTURED IN CHINA
10 9 8 7 6 5 4 3 2 1

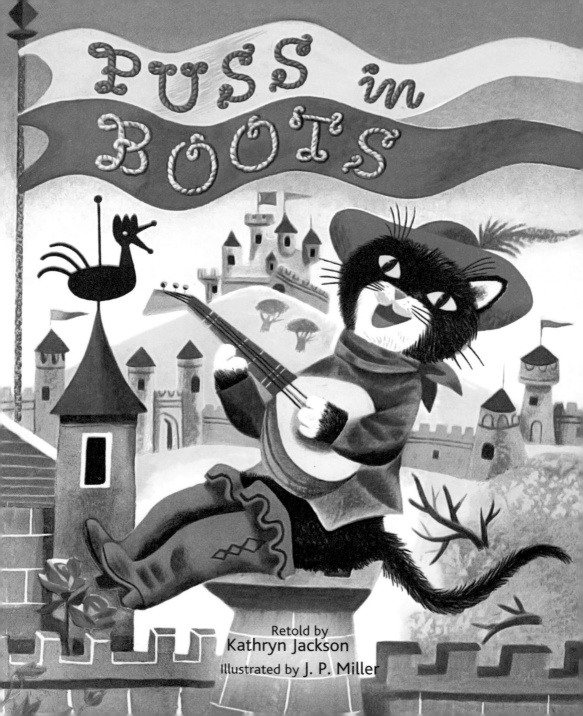

PUSS in BOOTS

Retold by
Kathryn Jackson

Illustrated by **J. P. Miller**

There was once a miller's youngest son whose father had left him nothing in all the world save a cat.

"How am I to live?" cried the poor lad. "With no more fortune than this, Puss and I are sure to starve!"

Now the cat, having heard his master's words, did not like the sound of them at all.

"Good master Caraba," said he, "only give me a pair of boots, a plumed hat, and an empty bag, and I will make you rich."

Caraba did as the cat asked.

And Puss, gallantly dressed in his fine new clothes, scooped a measure of grain into his bag and hurried off to the woods. There he quickly caught a rash young rabbit who came to eat the grain.

Puss went straight to the palace of the King.

Since the King liked nothing better than rabbit pie, Puss was soon bowing before him.

"My noble master, the Marquis of Carabas, sends you this gift," said he, "and with it the greetings of a loyal subject."

"Your master is most generous, Puss in Boots," the King replied.

The next day, Puss trapped two plump partridges and gave them to the King. Day after day, he brought some small game and presented it in the name of the Marquis of Carabas. And day after day, the King grew more curious about this noble Marquis!

At last one morning, he and his daughter
(the most beautiful Princess in all the world)
drove out to learn all they could about him.

No sooner did their coach turn toward the
river than Puss went running home as if his life
depended on it.

"Good master Caraba," he cried. "You must bathe
in the river at once!"

So great was his excitement that the miller's lad
did so, without asking why or wherefore.

And the moment he was in the water, Puss gathered up his dusty, shabby clothes, and hid them under a large rock.

Then, as the King's coach passed, out he ran, waving his arms and crying, "Help! Help! My master is drowning!"

The King remembered Puss in Boots well.

He sent his guards running to pull the astonished
Caraba out of the water.

While all this was going on, Puss told the King that some knave had stolen all his master's fine clothing and run off with it.

"Bring the Marquis of Carabas the finest suit in the palace," the King said to his master of the wardrobe.

This was soon done. And when the miller's lad had dressed in it, he was so handsome that the beautiful Princess looked at him once, and loved him with all her heart.

As for Caraba, he sat at her side wondering at her beauty, and wishing the ride might never end!

Puss, by this time, was running well ahead of the coach.

"All this land belongs to the Marquis of Carabas," he told the workers in the fields. "And any who deny it will be chopped as fine as herbs for the pot!"

So, each time the King leaned out to ask who owned the land, the frightened workers told him, "The Marquis of Carabas, and no other!"

While the King marveled at the richness of the land, Caraba marveled at his daughter's beauty and sweetness. And Puss, well pleased with himself, went running ahead to the castle of the wicked ogre who really owned all these fields.

He walked boldly through the great courtyard and the stately rooms, and at last he came upon the frightful ogre himself.

"I have heard," said Puss, looking far braver than he felt, "that you can turn yourself into a lion. But I cannot believe that even you can do that!"

"Can't you?" the ogre bellowed. In the twinkling of an eye, he had turned into a terrible, roaring lion, and back into an ogre again.

"Wonderful indeed!" cried Puss. "But I have also heard that great as you are, you can turn yourself into a tiny mouse. Surely this is not possible?"

"See for yourself!" roared the furious ogre. And at once he was a small gray mouse, scurrying across the floor.

This suited Puss perfectly. One pounce, and both mouse and ogre were gone forever.

Puss ran to the gates barely in time to throw them open for the royal coach.

"Welcome to the castle of my noble master, the Marquis of Carabas!" he cried.

When the King saw the richness and beauty of the castle, he was sure that the Marquis of Carabas was a proper young man indeed.

And after a magnificent feast that Puss had ordered prepared, he declared that no one but the noble Marquis was worthy of his daughter's hand!

Both Caraba and the Princess were overjoyed. Their wedding took place that very day.

And no one rejoiced more than Puss in Boots,
who lived with the Marquis and his beautiful bride
forever after.

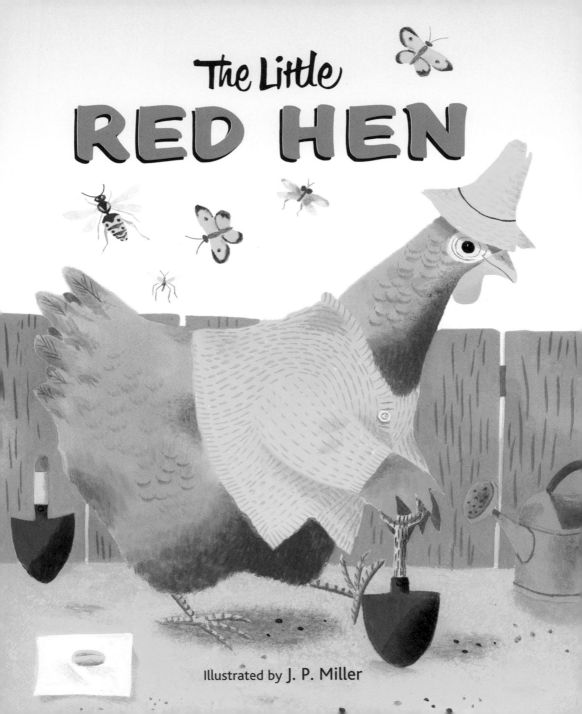

One summer day the Little Red Hen found a grain of wheat.

"A grain of wheat!" said the Little Red Hen to herself. "I will plant it."

She asked the duck:
"Will you help me plant this grain of wheat?"
"Not I!" said the duck.

She asked the goose:
"Will you help me plant this grain of wheat?"
"Not I!" said the goose.

She asked the cat:
"Will you help me plant this grain of wheat?"
"Not I!" said the cat.

She asked the pig:
"Will you help me plant this grain of wheat?"
"Not I!" said the pig.

"Then I will plant it myself," said the Little Red Hen. And she did.

Soon the wheat grew tall, and the Little Red Hen
knew it was time to reap it.

"Who will help me reap the wheat?" she asked.

"Not I!" said the duck.

"Not I!" said the goose.

"Not I!" said the cat.

"Not I!" said the pig.

"Then I will reap it myself,"
said the Little Red Hen.
And she did.

She reaped the wheat, and it was ready to be
taken to the mill and made into flour.

"Who will help me carry the wheat to the mill?"
she asked.

"Not I!" said the duck.
"Not I!" said the goose.
"Not I!" said the cat.
"Not I!" said the pig.

"Then I will carry it myself," said the Little Red
Hen. And she did. She carried the wheat to the mill,
and the miller made it into flour.

When she got it home, she asked, "Who will help
me make the flour into dough?"
"Not I!" said the duck.
"Not I!" said the goose.
"Not I!" said the cat.
"Not I!" said the pig.

"Then I will make the dough myself," said the
Little Red Hen. And she did.

Soon the bread was ready to go into the oven.

"Who will help me bake the bread?" said the
Little Red Hen.

"Not I!" said the duck.

"Not I!" said the goose.

"Not I!" said the cat.

"Not I!" said the pig.

"Then I will bake it myself," said the Little
Red Hen. And she did.

    After the loaf had been taken from the oven,
it was set on the windowsill to cool.

"And now," said the Little Red Hen, "who will help me eat the bread?"

"I will!" said the duck.

"I will!" said the goose.

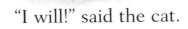

"I will!" said the cat.

"I will!" said the pig.

"No, I will eat it myself!" said the Little Red Hen. And she did.

the three bears

Illustrated by **Feodor Rojankovsky**

Once upon a time there were three bears—
a great big papa bear, a middle-sized mama bear,
and a wee little baby bear.

They lived in a little house in the forest.

They had three chairs—a great big chair for the papa bear, a middle-sized chair for the mama bear, and a wee little chair for the baby bear.

And upstairs there were three beds—a great big bed for the papa bear, a middle-sized bed for the mama bear, and a wee little bed for the baby bear.

One morning the mama bear made some porridge for breakfast.

She filled a great big bowl for the papa bear,
a middle-sized bowl for the mama bear, and a wee
little bowl for the baby bear.

But the porridge was too hot to eat, so the
three bears went out for a walk in the forest.

That same morning a little girl named Goldilocks was walking through the woods.

She came to the three bears' house. And she knocked on the door, but nobody called, "Come in." So she opened the door and went in.

Goldilocks saw the three chairs. She sat in the
great big chair. It was too hard. The middle-sized
chair was too soft. The baby chair was just right—
but it broke when she sat on it.

Now Goldilocks spied the porridge.
"I am hungry," she said.
So she tasted the porridge.
The porridge in the big bowl was too hot.

The porridge in the middle-sized bowl was too cold. The porridge in the wee little bowl was just right—so she ate it all up.

Then Goldilocks went upstairs and tried the beds.

The great big bed was too hard.

The middle-sized bed was too soft.
But the wee little bed was oh, so nice!
So Goldilocks lay down and went to sleep.

Then home through the forest and back to their house came the three bears—the great big bear, the middle-sized bear, and the wee little baby bear.

The moment they stepped into the house, they
saw that someone had been there.

"Humph!" said the papa bear in his great big
voice. "Someone has been sitting in my chair!"

"Land sakes!" said the mama bear in her middle-sized voice. "Someone has been sitting in *my* chair."

"Oh, dear!" cried the baby bear in his wee little voice. "Someone has been sitting in *my* chair, and has broken it all to bits."

Then they all looked at the table.

"Humph," said the papa bear in his great big voice. "Someone has been tasting my porridge."

"And someone has been tasting *my* porridge," said the mama bear.

"Someone has eaten *my* porridge all up," said
the baby bear sadly.

Then up the stairs went the three bears, with a thump-thump-thump, and a trot-trot-trot, and a skippity-skip-skip. (That was the wee little baby bear.)

"Humph," said the papa bear in his great big
voice. "Someone has been sleeping in my bed!"

"And someone has been sleeping in *my* bed,"
said the mama bear.

"Oh, dear!" cried the baby bear in his wee little
voice. "And someone has been sleeping in *my* bed,
and here she is right now!"

Goldilocks opened her eyes and she saw the
three bears.

"Oh!" said Goldilocks.

She was so surprised that she jumped right out
the window and ran all the way home.

And she never saw the house in the forest again.